Joan Lingard is the v[...]
numerous books for [...]
She was born in Edi[...]
now lives, but spent [...]
her life, from the age of two to eighteen, in
Belfast. Joan is married with three grown-
up daughters and one grandson.

Jacqui Thomas lives in East Sheen,
London with kids, cats, bicycles and one
grumpy car.

Clever Clive

Joan Lingard

Illustrated by Jacqui Thomas

Young Piper

PAN MACMILLAN

CHILDREN'S BOOKS

First published 1993 by Pan Macmillan Children's Books

This Young Piper edition published 1994 by Pan Macmillan Children's Books
a division of Pan Macmillan Publishers Limited
Cavaye Place London SW10 9PG
and Basingstoke

Associated companies throughout the world

ISBN 0 330 33292 9

Text copyright © 1993 Joan Lingard
Illustrations copyright © 1993 Jacqui Thomas

9 8 7 6 5 4 3 2 1

A CIP catalogue record for this book is available from
the British Library

Printed and bound in Great Britain by
Cox & Wyman Ltd, Reading, Berkshire

To Chloe
J. L.

To Mum and Dad Thomas
J. T.

Clive Clutterbuck's life changed the
day his Uncle Claude sent him a
pair of clogs.

"You won't remember your
Uncle Claude," said Clive's
mother, Mrs Clutterbuck. "He
went off to seek his fortune when
you were a baby."

"It says CLIVE on the soles," said
Mr Clutterbuck.

"That's why he bought them,"
said Mrs Clutterbuck. "It says so in
the letter."

Clive slipped his feet into the red
and yellow clogs. They felt soft and

smooth even though they were
made of wood. He did a little
dance.

Clip, clop, went the clogs,
clippety, clop!

Clive's baby sister, Chloe, beat in
time with her spoon. Bip, bop,
bippety, bop!

"What a clever boy you are!"
said Mr Clutterbuck.

Clive decided to take his clogs for a
walk. He clattered down the front
steps into the street.

Clip, clop, went the clogs,
clippety, clop.

Clive clumped into Mrs Shaw's
shop to buy a stick of clove rock.

Lucy Luckpenny and her mother
were at the counter.

"What nice clogs you've got,
Clive," said Lucy.

"I got them from my uncle in
Hawaii," said Clive.

"That'll be one pound twenty for the butter," said Mrs Shaw. "Seventy-seven pence for the sugar, and one fifty-five for the fish fingers."

"Three pounds fifty-two," said Clive before Mrs Shaw could ring it up on the till.

The next day Clive wore his clogs
to school. Everyone admired them.
   "Make sure they don't clatter too
much!" said Miss Timms the
teacher.

"Now class, what are six times nine?" she asked.

"Forty-five," shouted out Frankie Fairweather.

"Wrong, I'm afraid, Frankie," said Miss Timms. "Clive?"

fifty-four

"Correct, Clive."

"I bet he doesn't know what thirteen times thirteen are," muttered Frankie Fairweather.

"One hundred and sixty-nine," Clive answered as quick as a flash.

"Nineteen times nineteen?" asked Miranda Moon.

"Three hundred and sixty-one."

"Nineteen times three million and three?" asked Suzy Shaw.

"Fifty-seven million and fifty-seven."

The whole class gaped at Clive.

"Clive Clutterbuck thinks he knows everything," said Frankie Fairweather.

Clive was beginning to wonder if he did. He could answer every question that anyone asked.

"What is the heaviest snake in the world?"

"An anaconda!"

When Clive got home he went up
to his room. He sat on the bed and
stared at his feet.
Could his clogs
be magic clogs?
He decided to do
an experiment.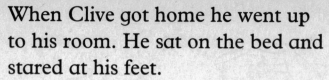

He took off the
clogs.

"Spell
rhinoceros!"
he told
himself.

"R-I-N – um –
O-S-S – er –
E-R-O-S,"
he spelled out.
He felt sure
that was
wrong.

He put the clogs back on.
Like lightning, he said the letters
straight out,

"R-H-I-N-O-C-E-R-O-S."

He felt sure that was right.

He did a little dance.

Clickety, click, clackety, clack, went the clogs as he clashed the heels together. Clive clapped his hands.

Now Frankie Fairweather was beginning to suspect Clive Clutterbuck's secret. He started to watch him.

One day, when some of the boys and girls were playing football in the park, Frankie stole Clive's clogs.

Frankie ran home. He went into his backyard and jumped into the clogs.

"Tell me what eleven times eleven are!" he demanded.

He waited. Nothing happened.

No answer came.

"You stupid old clumsy old clogs!" cried Frankie Fairweather, and threw them into the dustbin.

Clive was very upset when he couldn't find his clogs. He searched the park. His best friend Harry Hicks helped him look. And Lucy Luckpenny. And Miranda Moon. And Suzy Shaw.

They looked below the seats. And inside the litter bins.

And under the bushes.

"Perhaps they walked off on their own?" suggested Suzy Shaw.

They searched all the way home.

"You should be more careful, Clive," clucked his mother. "Fancy losing Uncle Claude's clogs!"

"That wasn't very clever, was it?" said Clive's father.

Clive hardly slept that night. He tossed and turned until the bedclothes were in a terrible tangle.

As soon as it was light he got up and went out into the back lane. It was dustbin morning.

Clive stood and thought. And then he remembered that Frankie Fairweather had run off from the park before anyone else.

He ran over to the Fairweathers'
bin and lifted the lid. He began to
rummage. He pulled out dented
tins and torn packets and crumpled
tin foil and a cracked cup and a
broken bread bin.

And then, right at the very bottom, covered with tea leaves, he found his red and yellow clogs!

Clive took the clogs home.

He washed and dried them. He took great care. Would his clogs still be clever clogs?

Just then the phone rang. Clive's mother answered it.

"You're going to live in Timbuktu? Where on earth is that?" she asked.

"Africa!" shouted Clive. "West Africa!"

"Come on!" said Suzy Shaw.

"There's nothing there!" cried Clive Clutterbuck.

"Only rubbish," said Suzy Shaw.

"Where do you find all these things?" asked Suzy Shaw.

"You wouldn't believe me if I told you."

"Try us," said Miranda Moon.

"Well, over there," said Lucy.

Mrs Shaw *was* pleased. She gave Lucy the biggest box of chocolates in the shop as a reward.

The other children in the street wished that they could be as lucky as Lucy Luckpenny.

"My goodness, Lucy!" Mrs
Shaw's eyes stood out, as if they
were on stalks. "It looks like my
grandmother's ring. She lost it
when I was a girl. *Wherever* did
you find it?"

"Up the street," said Lucy.

"Hello, Lucy," said Miranda.
"Where *have* you been?"

"I found a ring." Lucy opened
up her hand.

"A ring?" said Suzy Shaw.

"Let's have a look!" said
Mrs Shaw.

She picked it up. It was a ring. A golden ring, set with little sparkling diamonds and ruby red stones.

Lucy looped into the shop.

"Shut the door now, Lucy Luckpenny!" said Mrs Shaw in a sharp voice.

Lucy sat beside the fountain and
watched it playing.

When she turned her head,
something glittery caught her eye.
She went to see what this shiny
thing could be.

The next time the street was empty,
Lucy cartwheeled over the wall
again. It was grey and gloomy in
the street, but in the magic garden
the sun was shining.

Lucy went home and took out her orange. "Do you want a piece?" she asked Lily. It was the sweetest orange they had ever tasted.

"Where did you get it from?" asked Lily.

"Not telling." Lucy wasn't going to tell anyone where she had been, not even her best friend Miranda Moon.

"Up the street," said Lucy. It was true, wasn't it?

Mr Bumble *was* pleased. He gave Lucy fifty pence as a reward.

"It was lucky you were looking, Lucy," said Mr Bumble.

Then she sprang forward on to her hands and went flying back over the wall into the street.

Lucy went to call on Mr Bumble.

"I've found a watch, Mr Bumble."

"A watch, Lucy! This looks like my grandfather's watch. The one that I lost all those years ago. Good gracious me! *Wherever* did you find it?"

Suddenly something glittery caught her eye. The sun was striking it.

Lucy knelt down to see what it could be. It was a watch, an old-fashioned silver watch. She put it in her pocket.

She reached up and touched an
orange with her fingertips. It felt
warm from the sun. It fell plop into
the palm of her hand. She put it in
her pocket.

Lucy just sat and stared. She
wouldn't dare do loops in here. She
might crush the flowers or shake
the oranges and lemons from the
trees or frighten the birds.

A fountain played in the centre.
Flowers bloomed. Oranges and
lemons grew on sturdy little trees
with glossy green leaves. Birds with
bright feathers flitted in and out of
the branches.

Lucy found that she had landed in
the middle of a garden. She rested
a moment to get her breath back.

Then she looked around. "My
goodness!" she said. It was the
most wonderful garden Lucy had
ever seen.

At the end of the street, there was
a very high wall. This was the place
where Lucy usually stopped.

But today, she was flying so high
that she could not stop. She flew
straight over the top of the wall.

loop the loop just one more time?

She sprang forward on to her
hands and away she went, like a
whirling, birling top. Faster and
faster she went, faster and faster.
Higher and higher. She felt as if she
were flying.

Lucy looked up the lovely, long,
empty pavement. She longed to
cartwheel right down it.

She looked behind her. There
was nobody about. She looked in
front. Nobody there, either. What
harm would it do if she were to

said it was strange not to see Lucy
Luckpenny looping the loop.

Then came a day when the street
was very quiet. There was a special
football match on television and
everyone was inside watching it.

"Lucy, I think you've
got to stop doing cartwheels
in the street," said
Mr Luckpenny.
"She's always bumping
into people," said Lily.
So Lucy had to walk along
the street now. Everyone

"This is not my lucky day," he
said. "I lost my watch this
morning, too. I'm always losing
watches. Once I lost my
grandfather's watch. That was a
long time ago though."

"I'm very, very sorry," said
Lucy.

"Oh, goodness, Lucy!" cried Mrs Luckpenny.

Mr Luckpenny lifted Mr Bumble to his feet. Lucy's sister Lily picked up his shopping.

"I'm very sorry," said Lucy.

Mr Bumble was bumbling about looking bewildered.

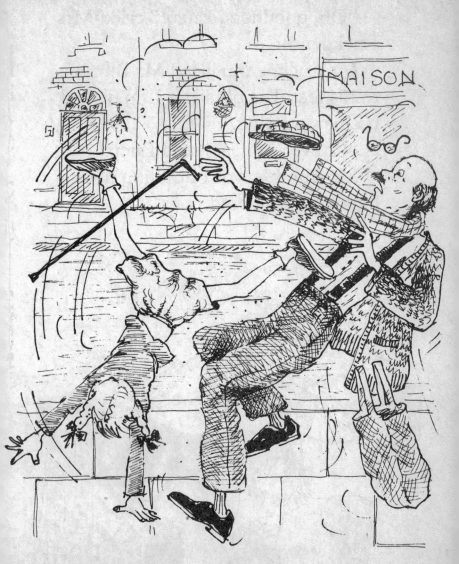

One day, when Lucy was
cartwheeling along the street, she
went careering into old Mr
Bumble.

"But I like looping the loop,"
said Lucy.

She looped so fast that she
looked like a spinning top.

"No cartwheels in my shop!"
said Mrs Shaw. "You could send
everything flying."

Lucy liked the feeling of flying.

Lucy Luckpenny was often called
Loopy Lucy. She did loops up and
down the street. She could do
forward loops, and she could do
backward loops.

"Why can't you walk upright?"
asked her mother Mrs Luckpenny.
"Like other children."

Loopy Lucy

Joan Lingard

Illustrated by Jacqui Thomas

Young Piper
PAN MACMILLAN
CHILDREN'S BOOKS